Forgiveness is a gift!

Carol Davis

I HOPE YOU'LL BE A FAN OF DEECEE!

Jan Raanan

No part of this publication may be reproduced in whole or in part, or stored in a retrieval system without written permission of the publisher.

Library of Congress Catalog Number: 2016952945

ISBN 978-0-9905985-1-0

Register of Copyrights, United States of America

Copyright 2017 by From Door to Door Publishing.

All rights reserved.

Printed in the U.S.A.

It was the end of October
and the wind blew cold.

DeeCee the freighter was coming home
to Wisconsin, she was told.

DeeCee was built in Sturgeon Bay,
So she was excited to come this way

To see her friends after working so hard
on the Great Lakes nearly every day.

The days finally came when Old Man Winter
made it hard to move a freighter.

DeeCee needed to find the place
to be fixed up – to be even greater.

When she came into the shipyard
no friends were there,

Only large freighters
who warned her to "Beware."

DeeCee tried to make friends each day,
But those crabby freighters only pushed her away.

DeeCee was the smallest of the freighters,
They kept bumping her out of line.

They wanted all the attention
to be fixed first – or else they started to whine.

DeeCee was O so sad
and knew not what to do.

She expected this to be such fun,
And now felt very blue.

The next day a storm blew in mighty hard.

The snow was a-flying all over the dockyard.

It got mighty cold and the ice froze hard.

The big freighters stuck in the big shipyard.

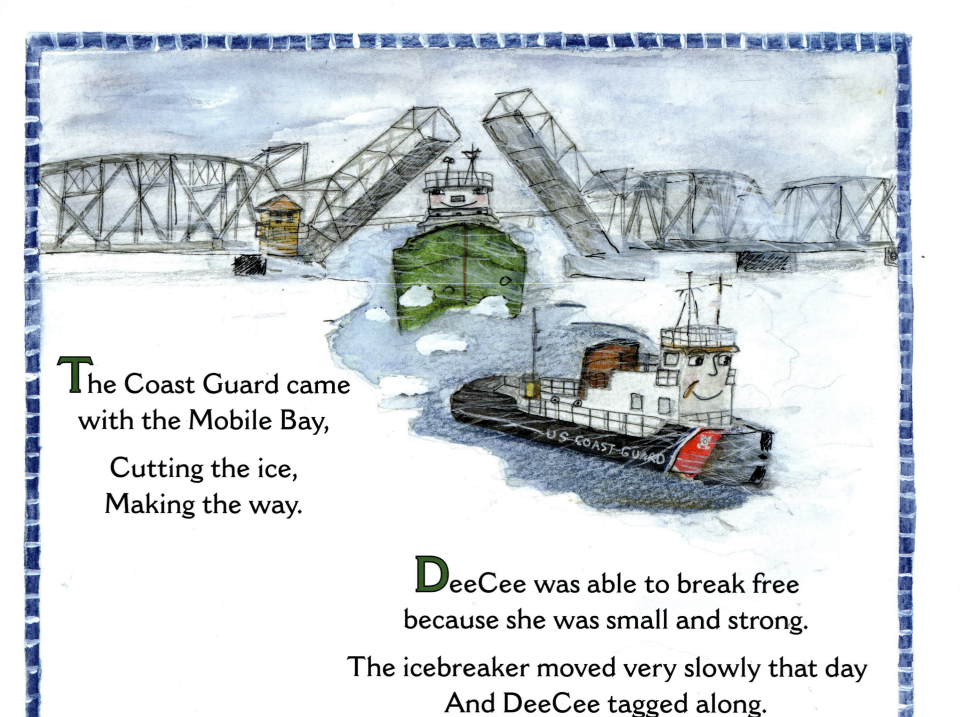

The Coast Guard came with the Mobile Bay,

Cutting the ice,
Making the way.

DeeCee was able to break free because she was small and strong.

The icebreaker moved very slowly that day
And DeeCee tagged along.

A call for help came one day:
Washington Island was frozen in.

They needed food and gas and things,
Their supplies were running thin.

Another call went out to freighters
to bring the needed supplies.

To the islands all around,
Only DeeCee was mobilized.

They filled her up to the brim,
She sat low in the water.

Ice, snow, wind and hail
scared other freighters – not her.

DeeCee followed the Mobile Bay,
Ice hitting the ship all around.

She was scratched from stem to stern
but she would never back down.

DeeCee made it to the islands,
People cheered for the ship.

Then they unloaded boxes and things
and were grateful she had made the trip.

DeeCee came back a big hero that day,
She delivered supplies all around.

Everyone was safe and thankful to her
in each little island town.

The big cranky freighters
were embarrassed once more,

Knowing they had picked
on this little eye sore.

DeeCee was painted
to look brand new.

The other freighters allowed her
to pass right though.

DeeCee made many friends that day,
Now they wanted to have fun and play.

DeeCee forgave them
And shouted "Hooray!"

BEACHBALL   FREIGHTER BEACHBALL

Now DeeCee is back to work.
She thinks of the day of all the snowflakes.

One important lesson learned:
Forgive each other – we all make mistakes!!

Words of Explanation:

Lake freighters, or lakers – are bulk carrier vessels that ply the Great Lakes of North America. These vessels are traditionally called boats, although classified as ships. Lakers carry bulk cargoes of materials such as limestone, iron ore, grain, coal or salt from the mines and fields to the populous industrial areas down the lakes. The 63 commercial ports handled 173 million tons of cargo in 2006. Because of winter ice on the lakes, the navigation season is not usually year-round… From mid-January to late March, most boats are laid up for maintenance. Crewmembers spend these months ashore. – Wikipedia.org

Fincinteri Bay Shipbuilding – Tracing its history back to 1918, and located in Sturgeon Bay, WI, Fincantieri Bay Shipbuilding (FBS) is an industry leader in the construction and repair of large ships. The FBS portfolio includes OPA 90-compliant vessels, dredges and dredging support equipment, and offshore support vessels. On the repair side, FBS is expert at managing critical deadlines in the repair and sustainment of the Great Lakes Winter Fleet. Parent company, FINCANTIERI, has recently completed a $26 million capital expansion plan for the FBS facility including a new floating drydock, computer-aided manufacturing equipment, and climate-controlled manufacturing facilities. history back to 1918, and located in Sturgeon Bay, WI, Fincantieri Bay Shipbuilding (FBS) is an industry leader in the construction and repair of large ships. The FBS portfolio includes OPA 90-compliant vessels, dredges and dredging support equipment, and offshore support vessels. On the repair side, FBS is expert at managing critical deadlines in the repair and sustainment of the Great Lakes Winter Fleet. Parent company, FINCANTIERI, has recently completed a $26 million capital expansion plan for the FBS facility including a new floating drydock, computer-aided manufacturing, and climate-controlled manufacturing facilities. – http://www.bayshipbuildingcompany.com/profile.html

To learn more about Great Lakes maritime industry and history – you can visit the Door County Maritime Museum. – www.dcmm.org

Washington Island – Washington Island, WI, located six miles off the tip of the Door County Peninsula, is a favorite Midwest destination for tourists year-round. People come to Washington Island to get away from the tension of urban life, to travel "North of the Tension Line" and enjoy a slower, relaxing pace of life. – http://www.washingtonisland.com

US Coast Guard – The U.S. Coast Guard is one of the five armed forces of the United States and the only military organization within the Department of Homeland Security. Since 1790 the Coast Guard has safeguarded our Nation's maritime interests and environment around the world. The Coast Guard is an adaptable, responsive military force of maritime professionals whose broad legal authorities, capable assets, geographic diversity and expansive partnerships provide a persistent presence along our rivers, in the ports, littoral regions and on the high seas. Coast Guard presence and impact is local, regional, national and international. These attributes make the Coast Guard a unique instrument of maritime safety, security and environmental stewardship. – https://www.uscg.mil/top/about

We love our Coasties in Sturgeon Bay!!

The Sturgeon Bay Bridge – (known as the Michigan Street Bridge) is a historic bridge in Sturgeon Bay, Wisconsin, United States. The bridge was built in 1929 and opened July 4, 1931, with a grand parade where it was officially dedicated as a Door County Veterans Memorial which plaques at either end still reads "To honor those who gave of themselves, to their country, in times of need" as a gift by the State of Wisconsin. The bridge carried Maple and Michigan Streets traffic, which was signed as Wisconsin Business Highway 42/57. The Sturgeon Bay Bridge was listed on the National Register of Historic Places on January 17, 2008. https://en.wikipedia.org/wiki/Sturgeon_Bay_Bridge#cite_ref-wisdot_12-0 – Wikipedia

Forgiveness – Forgiveness starts with a decision within your heart. If someone has wronged you, you may be angry or upset. Those feelings will tend to stay with you until you let go of those feelings and forgive the person who has done you wrong. It doesn't always happen quickly. Forgiveness isn't letting the other person 'off the hook' to continue to be able to hurt other people or you again. We may not be friendly with them or go back to the old relationship. While God commands us to forgive others as He forgave us, He never told us to keep trusting those who violated our trust or even to like being around them. Forgiving is about your heart attitude- letting go of your bitterness – while remembering very clearly your rights to healthy boundaries. Forgiveness helps you to lead a healthier life.

For more information: http//www.focusonthefamily.com/forgiveness

To help celebrate Door County, we have hidden a small door with a spiral door knob in each picture page within this book. Have fun looking for all the Doors!

Carol Davis lives with her wonderful husband, Steve and feels blessed to live in such a beautiful place as Door County, WI. Carol is a grief counselor and has published two other books. They have four children, three in WI, one in MD. They are blessed to have three handsome grandsons! She enjoys being outdoors, writing, reading and sewing. She believes in forgiveness and how that can change one's life....

"I dedicate this book to my husband Steve who came up with this story. Thank you Honey for 37 years of marriage and love and great stories! I love you!"

Jan Rasmussen was born and raised in Racine. She went to college in Wichita, Kansas, and later moved to Green Bay. In 2000, God brought her through a series of circumstances that were very difficult at the time, but led she and her family to move to Door County. Sixteen years later, there is nowhere they'd rather be.

"Dedicated with endless gratitude and love to Terry Stephens. She was an amazing person, who always found hope in people and situations when no one else could. She lived out her faith with kindness, grace, humor and generosity. She made the world a better place every day she was in it."